This Poppy's Tail book belongs to

....

For Ernest,
with love,

Cate Douglas
♡

For Anna

First published in Great Britain in 2017 by Bobbun Books Ltd.

160 Sutherland Avenue, London W9 1HP.

www.bobbunbooks.com

Text and illustrations copyright © Cate Douglas 2017.

The right of Cate Douglas to be identified as the author and illustrator of this work

has been asserted in accordance with the Copyright, Designs and Patents Act 1988.

ISBN 978-1-9997192-0-3

A CIP catalogue record for this book is available from the British Library.

Printed in the U.K.

Poppy's Tail

Cate Douglas

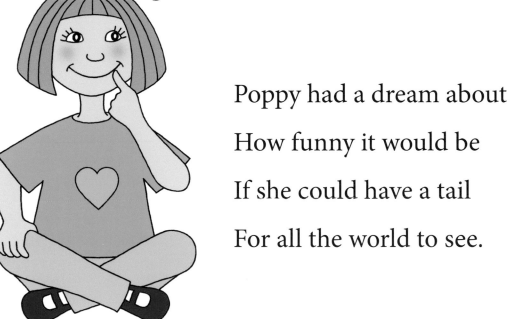

Poppy had a dream about

How funny it would be

If she could have a tail

For all the world to see.

It could be bushy like a squirrel

Or skinny like a rat

Curly like a piglet

Or silky like a cat.

It could be stripy like a tiger

Or plain—in black

—or white

Spotty like a leopard

In shades of dark and light.

It could be feathered like a peacock

Or flowing like a horse

And she could even plait it
To look extra smart of course.

It could be spiky like a crocodile

Or scaly like a fish

Fluffy like a bunny

Or one that she could swish.

But Poppy thinks a rainbow tail
Could be tremendous fun

This multicoloured dazzler
Would astonish everyone!

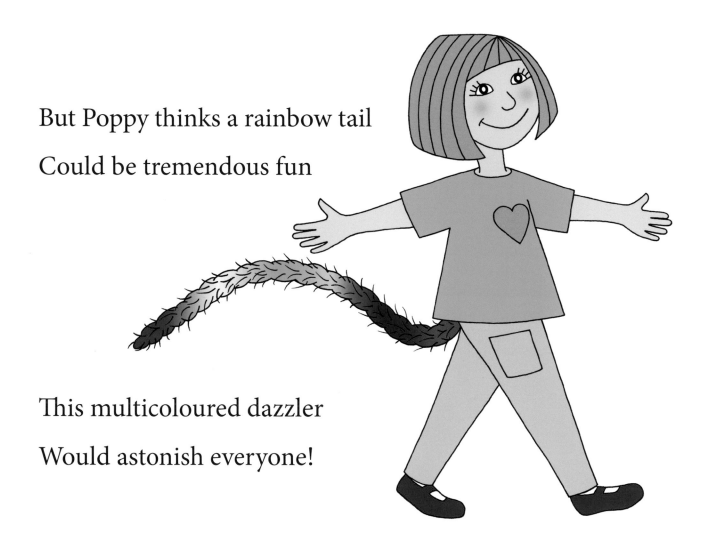

She'd waggle it from left to right

And swirl it round and round

Point it high up in the air

Or trail it on the ground.

With it dangling on her shoulder

She'd strike a stunning pose

And it would come in handy

For a tickle on her nose!

She could dress it to look pretty

With a fancy velvet bow

And in a beauty contest

She'd surely steal the show.

In summer she could use it
As a fan to keep her cool

Or as a scarf in winter
When on her way to school.

She'd pop a sock upon the end

To stop it getting cold

And at Christmas add some tinsel

In silver or in gold.

Now if it were especially long

She'd tie it in a knot

To serve as a reminder

Of something she forgot.

But best of all she'd use it

To set a brand new trend …

For giving furry tail-hugs

To all her tailless friends.

Then when the day is over

And it's time to go to bed

She'd snuggle down all cosy

With it curled around her head.

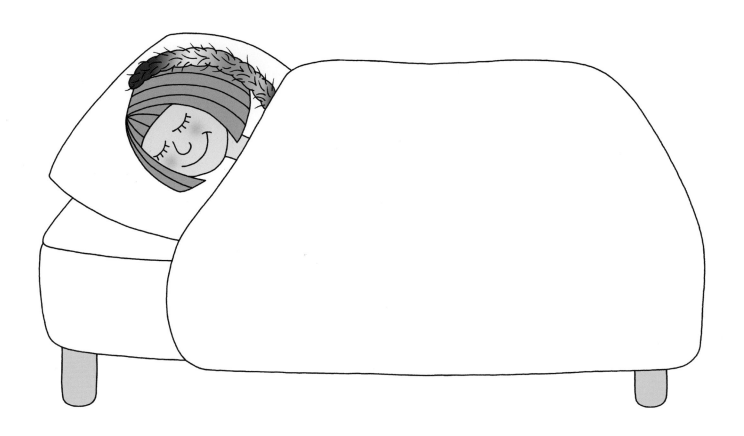

Good night Poppy!